Santa
Doesn't Need
Your Help

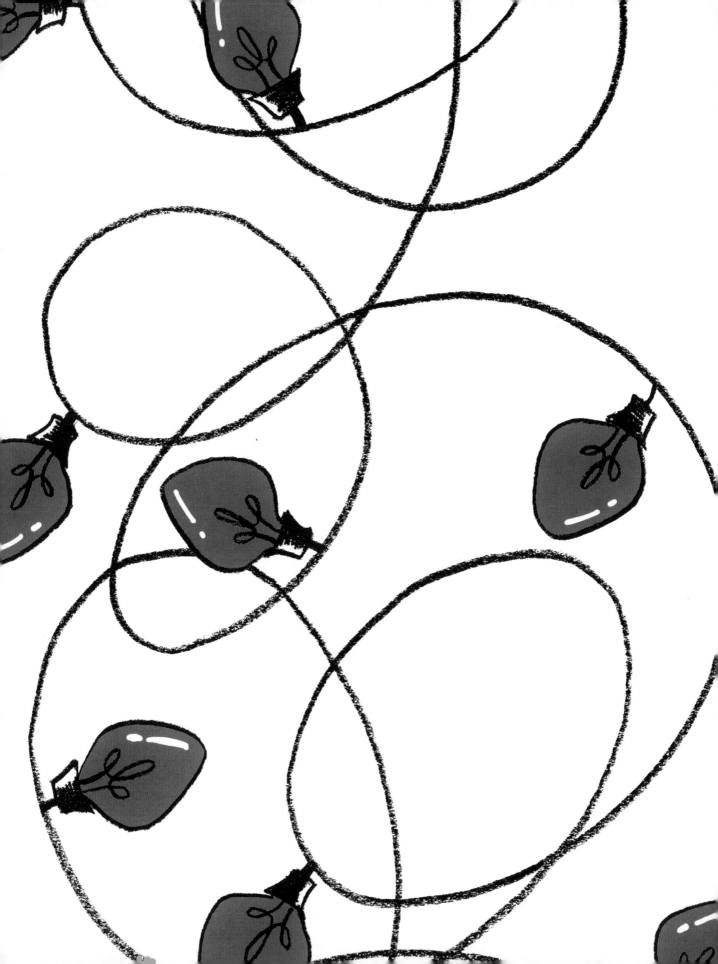

Santa
Doesn't Need
Your Help

Kevin
Maher

Illustrated By Joe
Dator

TURNER
PUBLISHING COMPANY

Turner Publishing Company
Nashville, Tennessee
www.turnerpublishing.com

Cover and book design by Joe Dator

Library of Congress Control Number: 2022941679

Hardcover 9781684429165
Paperback 9781684429158
Ebook 9781684429172

Printed in Canada

For Rebecca—K.M.

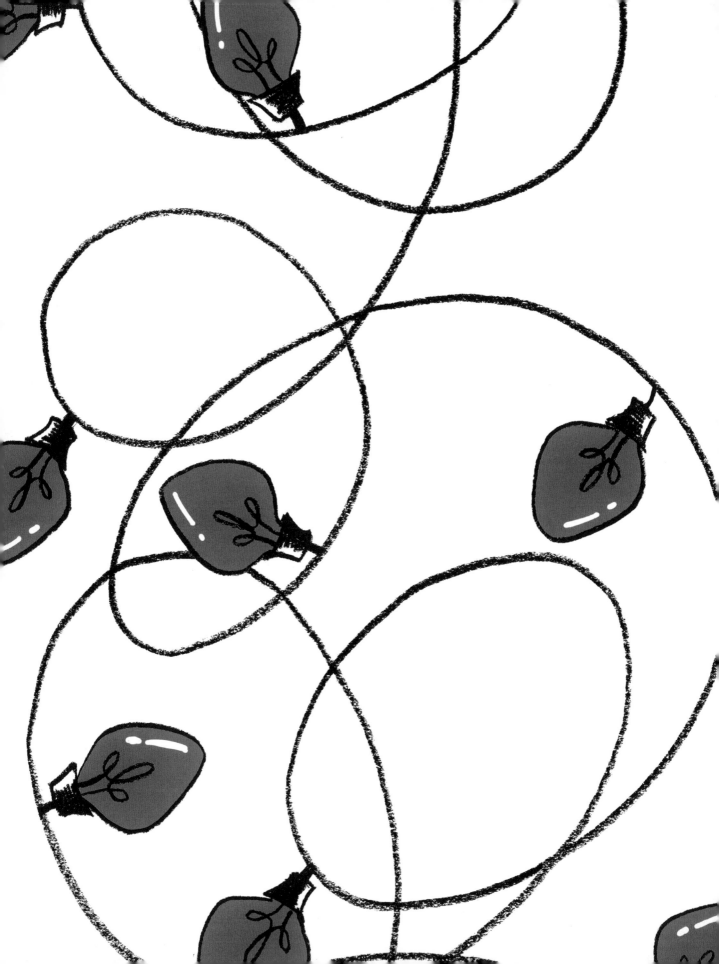

The workshop was busy, the tension was mounting,

'Cause Christmas was coming, just two days and counting!

All the toys had been built, almost ready to go,
Soon those presents would travel
through rain, sleet, or snow.

Now all that was left
was the final gift wrappin',

When something surprising
and wonderful happened.

A chopper flew in
with an entrance so grand–

And out came a world-famous K-Pop Boy band.

The boys had an idea that was met with applause:

This year *they* could step in
to replace Santa Claus.

"We'll go out tomorrow
with sleigh and reindeer,

Deliver the presents, save Christmas this year!"

The elves shouted **"Hooray!"**
and they high fived a lot.

Yes, the workshop was happy . . .

but Santa was not.

It happens like clockwork on Santa's big day.

They wear his red hat, push him out of the way.

They come from all over, they travel up north.

They take
Santa's place on
December 24th.

Grab his
presents and
sled, and
then quickly
they leave

To pretend they
were Santa Claus on
Christmas Eve.

Yes, Christmas gets "saved" by someone each December,

Far too many Santas, too many to remember.

Now St. Nick sensed a pattern he could not ignore:
"Do people think I can't do my job anymore?"

"I **DON'T** need your help!"
Santa got mad and yell-y.

His gut
shook like
a bowl full
of furious
jelly!

Santa sent the band home,
their heads bowed, feeling humble,

Then he turned to the elves
and groaned a grumpy grumble.

"I don't tell **YOU** how to work–"
he started to say.

Truth is he micromanaged the elves every day.

"Bah! I'm going to bed,"
he stormed off with a frown,
"Not because I'm too old, I just want to lie down."

But lying in bed, Santa could not escape
the feeling that he'd made
an awful mistake.

Was he getting too old?
Was it time to retire?
He dozed off while counting
the flames in the fire.

And when Christmas Eve came,
he was ready to go!

But a few minor things,
made him move a bit slow.

His eyeballs felt dizzy,
his gall bladder ached,

His tongue felt like five pounds
of moldy fruitcake.

Both his earlobes felt bloated, his shoulders were tight,
His pancreas, somehow, just didn't feel right.

There were cramps in his knees,
his buttocks were clenched,

He had pains in his beard
and his armpits were drenched.

His throat had a tickle; all the aches were non-stop,

When he moved his elbow, it went
snap, crackle, pop!

His feet felt too hot, and his vision was blurry . . .

"No big deal," grinned Saint Nick,
"there's no reason to worry."

It's probably nerves,
yes, I'm sure this will pass.

Might be something I ate,
or maybe just gas."

"There's just a few hours to accomplish my vow.

I've got to get going, and I've got to go now!"

"On Dasher, on Dancer, on Cupid, on Comet,
I must show the whole world that Santa's still got it!"

Just outside of Paris, Santa got excited,
The flame was rekindled, that old spark ignited.

He soared over houses and raced over streets,
Santa got his groove back, not losing a beat.

The sweetness of cookies, the fresh scent of trees,

Ah, the magic of moonlight—what a fine Christmas Eve!

Giving out all those presents
to good girls and good boys:

Games, dolls, and drum kits–
bikes, balls, and toys.

But then, a disaster you might not believe
Struck poor ol' Saint Nick
on the streets of Belize.

By the north side of
Main Street, just west of
Broadway,

MAIN ST

BROADWAY

Santa could've sworn . . .

that was where he'd parked the sleigh.

"Maybe it was stolen,
could be it was thieves,

Could be there's a tow truck
working late on Christmas Eve."

Santa made excuses,
even blamed things on an elf,
The only one he didn't fault
was Santa Claus, himself.

"Hey Boss!" Blitzen yelled.
"Over here. You okay?"

They were across the street . . .
They must have run away.

Hence Christmas Eve continued,
without another hitch,

Till they got to Denver,
where there was a minor glitch.

Little Lucy Rogers,
age seven (almost eight),

Wanted to see Santa,
so she stayed up late.

What she saw surprised her,
she thought it was a gag:

A droopy old Saint Nick who couldn't
even lift his bag?

"Santa, do you need help?
That prob'ly weighs a lot."

"No, I don't need **your** help.
I certainly do not!"

"I am not an invalid.
Can't you all understand?
Santa doesn't need your help.
Let me be a man!"

Then he kept on struggling,
and didn't say goodbye,

Careful not to swear with
a child so close by.

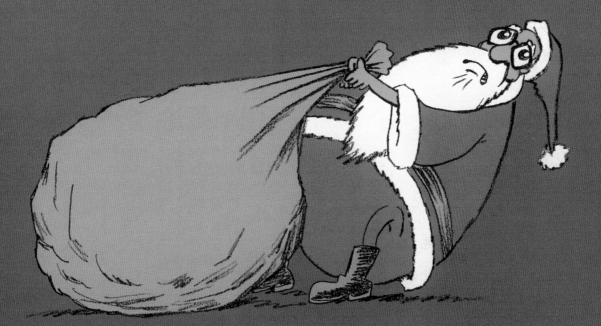

Stumbling, fumbling, grumbling—
and a bit of grieving.

Finally, he had it—
at last he was leaving!

After that big failure,
Santa felt defeated.

Still he would not admit that *any* help
was needed.

Santa picked up the pace,
with three hours remaining,
Still, the setbacks increased—
embarrassing and draining.

He stubbed his
little toe, he
banged his big
old head,

Fell down in a hallway,
almost crushed a dog
named Fred.

He woke a sleeping baby, knocked over some plants.

He farted in a fireplace (and almost pooped his pants).

He suffered several detours—
which took a bit of time—

In total, Santa stopped to pee forty-seven times.

Finally came Portland,
'twas the worst stop, no doubt.

He went into a chimney . . .
but then could not get out.

Trapped in a brick prison,
anxious to his core,

This never had happened
to old Saint Nick before!

Forty minutes, now lost—
it rattled Santa Claus,

Alone with his thoughts
in this unexpected pause.

He looked back on his life—
and contemplated death.

Finally, he calmed down
and focused on his breath.

He found it oddly peaceful and
even somewhat strange . . .

"But if I get out of this, I promise things will change!"

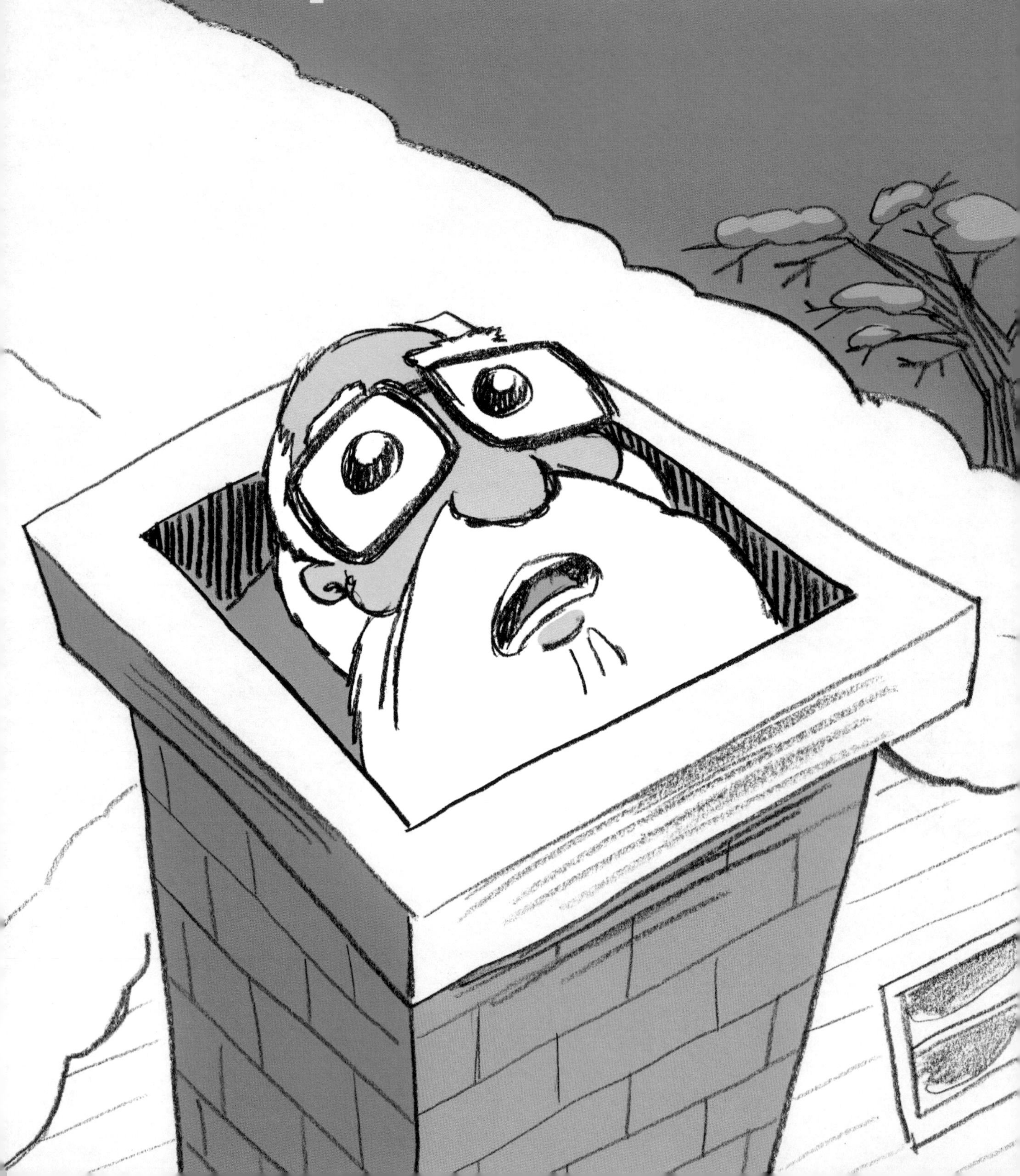

Santa felt his years now,
and let out a big sigh.

He acknowledged his age,
and had a real good cry.

He'd refused any help, to avoid looking weak,

"And that was a mistake–
'cause now I'm up the creek!"

Through a river of tears, he cried,
"Christmas is ruined!

Because I was too proud!
This was all my doin'!"

But those tears soaked the bricks,
helping Santa's descent,

And the next thing he knew,
down the chimney he went!

To the floor with a splash,
now released from confinement,

He was free to get on with
his Christmas assignment.

That's when Santa realized
(as he let out a yelp):

It's okay to get old,
it's okay to get help.

Santa called for backup,
and they took to the skies,

Those last presents delivered,
just before sunrise.

Once the job was finished,
the last gifting performed,

Mr. Claus traveled home;
a little bit transformed.

He had learned a lesson,
here's the moral condensed:

The greatest gift of all may
be self-acceptance.

So please, be kind to Santa—
and show some empathy—
If you get the wrong
gift underneath your
Christmas tree.

STEAK KNIVES

BATTERY

The End

About the Author

Kevin Maher is an Emmy-nominated writer, filmmaker, comedian, and poet. His work has been featured on AMC, Comedy Central, and Nickelodeon. His short films have been shown everywhere from MOMA to Troma, with screenings outside of Sundance and Cannes. Kevin directed the one-man show **I, SANTA: Confessions from Behind the Beard** and has worked as a Santa-for-hire. He lives in New York with his wife and two sons. To see his videos, visit www.LoveKevin.com.

About the Illustrator

Joe Dator has been a cartoonist for the **New Yorker** since 2006 and has also contributed cartoons to **MAD** magazine and **Esquire**. He is a recipient of the National Cartoonists Society's Silver Reuben Award and has been featured on CBS's **60 Minutes**. In 2021, he published a collection of his work titled **INKED: Cartoons, Confessions, Rejected Ideas and Secret Sketches from the New Yorker's Joe Dator**. In addition to cartooning, he has presented humorous lectures on everything from Japanese movie monsters to fictitious comedy albums and is the co-host of the Comedy Film Funnel podcast. He lives in New York City.

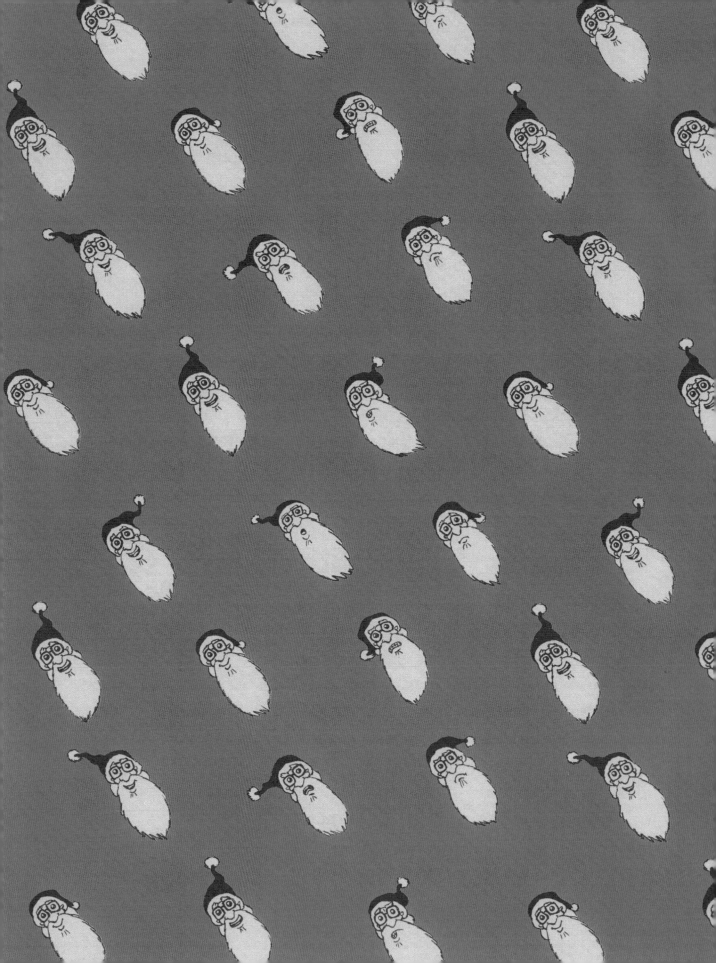